ENCHANTAILS™

MARIANA

Tasi
and the Danger of the Deep

Published by Marshall Jones Company
Los Lunas, New Mexico

Based on the characters and universe created by Mark & Tristy Viniello

This is a work of fiction. Literary perceptions and insights are based on experience. All names, characters, places, and incidents are either products of the author's imagination or are used fictitiously. No reference to any real person is intended or should be inferred.

Library of Congress Control Number: 2015920608

ISBN 978-0-8338-0244-6

ENCHANTAILS: Mariana Realm Series: Book 1
10-9-8-7-6-5-4-3-2-1
First Edition

Manufactured in the United States of America.

Manufactured by Thomson-Shore, Dexter, MI (USA); RMA10LS782, March, 2016

ENCHANTAILS™

Tasi
and the Danger of the Deep

Written by Heather E. Carson
Based on characters and universe created by Mark & Tristy Viniello
Illustrations by Alliance Studio
Cover and interior design by Ken Raney

Marshall Jones Company
Publishers Since 1902
Los Lunas, New Mexico

MARIANA

CONTENTS

1

A Bit of Sparkle

There!" she said with satisfaction. Tasi lifted her goggles up onto her fiery red hair and set down her welding torch. She had just finished putting finishing touches on the door hinge for old Mrs. Chow, who floated over for a closer look.

Mrs. Chow opened and closed the door several times, noticing that the hinge glided perfectly. But there was something else. "What is that?" Mrs. Chow asked with a touch of criticism.

Tasi could see Mrs. Chow's bony finger pointing at the *bioluminescent* sea moss stuffed into the hinge joint. "Oh, that is just a bit of sparkle that will light up the threshold when you open the door," Tasi cheerfully explained. "It will help you see where you are going."

"I'll have you know I have lived here for more than half a sea cycle and I do just fine without...

TASI

sparkle." Mrs. Chow swam into her dwelling and closed the door effortlessly behind her.

Tasi chuckled. She couldn't help but make things beautiful. She hoped in her heart that, even though they rarely said it, her neighbors felt secretly happy with her special touches. Most of the merfolk in her realm didn't understand art. They always were focusing on function.

Tasi packed her tools into her satchel and headed back to her Form and Function class. She was ever so grateful for the community assignments that got her out of class once in awhile. Tasi was not one to sit still.

She couldn't help but pause for a moment as she swam up and over one of the *Mìmì Qiáo*, the secret bridges that connected various parts of the city. Before her lay the most magnificent realm in the sea. *Mariana* glowed with the industrious sparks of the metal-workers. The realm was a maze of elaborate structures, made strong from the iron, copper and silver that was plentiful there.

Every one of merfolk took pride in making Mariana strong. Certain parts of this massive realm descended over 35,000 feet into the blackest deep. They contained mysteries that remained hidden from even the bravest Mariana explorers and their precious records.

Tasi proudly scanned the city until her eyes fell upon the towering spires of the castle rising out of the *Shēn* in its center.

TASI

The castle, called *Zhēnzhū*, was truly the most amazing structure in the realm. It was designed from the remnants of sunken ships by the kings themselves who had a special talent for architecture. Engineering ran in their royal veins. The King was renowned for his vision and craftsmanship. He hoped his genius would be passed on to one of his heirs.

Remembering that made Tasi's spirit fall. She was the King's oldest daughter, a beautiful and inventive redhead with a long tail of deep, iridescent, purple scales. But, at 15, Tasi had yet to prove she had the gift. Her grades in Form and Function class were not that great. She just couldn't get excited about building. She would much rather decorate and embellish and make things unique. Not very many merfolk cared about that, as Mrs. Chow had pointed out.

Tasi noticed a group of *Collectors* heading to the outskirts of the realm. Her green eyes lit up. "Maybe they are going to that shipwreck Kelix told me about!"

She swam closer to get a better look. Sure enough, the royal guards, called *"Cerberi,"* were accompanying the Collectors. That only occurred when they were going some place dangerous.

Tasi's friend Kelix was one of the Cerberi. She could see him in the ranks. He was a tall merboy with scales that glistened like polished steel. He had a mop of dark hair that was always hanging in his eyes unless it was stuffed inside his helmet. He looked so serious today, Tasi wanted to bust out laughing. She knew how goofy Kelix could be, especially when he was excited about a new adventure.

Tasi, in her memory, could still hear Kelix going on and on about this new discovery. "It is bigger than any ship they've discovered in years," he had told her, his eyes wild with enthusiasm. "They think it is like 3,000 years old, which means it may contain the treasures of land kings."

Tasi remembered being totally dazzled by Kelix's tale. He had told her land kings were obsessed with gold and knew how to carve amazing things out of it. They also loved the hides, shells and teeth of land creatures.

"These treasures would blow your mind, Tasi," Kelix had said. "Jewelry and sculptures made out of gorgeous stones not found in our realm and tusks bigger than the ones given to your father from the Arctic King!"

Tasi knew she was not supposed to venture into the outer realm by herself, let alone skip class. But seeing Kelix and remembering his exciting tales made her forget all about the rules. She had to see this shipwreck for herself.

Tasi took a special brass compass out of her satchel and excitedly opened the lid. The compass began to glow immediately. Tasi could see the direction the Collectors were heading. They were setting off to *Hǎinán Wān*, better known as Shipwreck Bay. She was delighted!

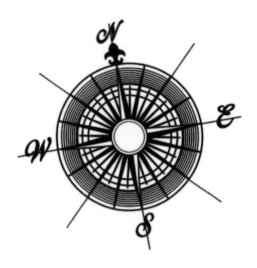

2
What a Wreck!

Tasi followed the Collectors at a safe distance, so they wouldn't notice her until they reached the giant hull of a great ship. Her imagination quickly turned to thoughts of the exciting pirate and war ships prized by the Collectors that always found their way into the bedtime stories of Mariana merfolk. She could see this ship was different as she got closer.

"Kelix was right! It's a cargo ship," she thought to herself. There would be many artifacts inside she could use in her creations back home.

The leader of the Collectors turned towards Tasi just then, causing her to quickly duck behind the barnacle-covered rocks and hold her breath. The leader's name was Fān. She was 18 and had been the head of her class. Fān was also strong and pretty. She hated Tasi for some unknown reason, and was always trying to get her in trouble. But, thankfully Fān was focused on giving instructions to her group and didn't catch a glimpse of Tasi's red curls floating above the rocks.

The Collectors joined hands and chanted the Realm motto together: *"Find the Lost."* They then split up to search the ship's hull. The Cerberi spread themselves out between the ship and the open water to protect the Collectors.

Tasi realized from her position at the back of the ship she could easily dart over and slip between the rotting boards without being noticed. She bravely counted to three and made a dash for it.

Tasi could not believe her eyes once she was inside. The cargo ship was filled with incredible treasures. She saw metals, such as copper and tin, which she knew the Collectors would be after. They were charged with finding valuable building materials. But Tasi was more interested in the fragments of ebony, shiny glass and amber beads.

"This ship must have belonged to the land kings," Tasi reasoned, as she gathered the treasures in her satchel.

Then, she spotted a giant spike of ivory wedged between some of the planks. "A tusk!" Tasi gasped. "Kelix is not going to believe this," she said out loud. Her mind began to race with thoughts of the creations she could make with that.

She quickly swam over and began to pull with all her might. The tusk came loose slowly, but with

it, the planks began to give way. The entire space she was in suddenly began to collapse.

Tasi left the tusk behind and swam frantically toward the opening. The Collectors would not be able to catch her if she could slip out now. She might even be able to make it back to the city unnoticed.

Something familiar caught her eye. It was a fleeting glow in the dark water. Tasi immediately knew what it was – a rare tiger tail seahorse that happened to be her best friend, *Copper*.

Tasi turned back and wrapped herself around the tiny seahorse instead of escaping. The compartment came crashing down around them, kicking up a cloud of murky dust from the depths. Tasi and Copper miraculously were not crushed. But when the dust settled, they found themselves surrounded by angry Collectors and Cerberi. Tasi caught the horrified look on Kelix's face as he realized who had caused the collapse. Fān swooped in with a superior smirk.

"Behold, my fellow Collectors. It seems the collapse wasn't an accident at all," Fān harshly announced. "We were being sabotaged by a mermaid who has no business in these waters."

Kelix swam forward in Tasi's defense. "Tasi is a royal daughter," he said, reminding Fān to show respect.

"But even a princess is not above the law," Fān announced with polite authority. "Anyone who interferes with work that strengthens our realm is subject to punishment."

Fān quickly picked up an echo shell. These were used by the Merfolk to hold and transport messages, just as shells on land still hold the voice of the sea. Fān quickly spoke her charges into the shell and handed it to one of the guards. "Take this to the palace, immediately."

"No," Tasi began to protest. But Fān quickly interrupted, swimming close to Tasi's face to rub it in. "Not even a royal daughter will be able to get out of this one," she whispered. Fān then ordered the Cerberi to escort Tasi back to the castle for punishment. "Return the princess to our King!"

TASI

3

On the Hook

Tasi hung her head. The Cerberi and Collectors surrounded her, so she knew there was nothing she could do but give in to Fān's accusations. Kelix quickly volunteered to escort Tasi back to the castle, hoping he might be able to reason with the King. He took Tasi by the arm and lead her away.

Kelix relaxed his grip once they were beyond the bay. "Tasi, what were you thinking?" he asked.

"You made this shipwreck sound so incredible, I just had to see it for myself," she explained. "Oh my gosh, I found the coolest stuff in there." Tasi reached into her bag to show off the amber beads.

"You could have been crushed!" Kelix reminded her. "Copper, too."

Tasi turned to her sweet and trustworthy Sea Buddy. "I should have known you would have been following me."

Sea horses are silent and majestic creatures, but
Copper wanted to show Tasi he was just fine. So, he
zigged and zagged energetically in the water. Tasi
reached out to inspect the armor she had crafted
for her tiny friend. "Your bioluminescence appears
to be running low. Come here and let me…" Tasi
stopped short, when she noticed that Kelix was
watching closely. "We can fix that when we get
back," she said. "But thank goodness it was there,
or I never would have seen you, you sneaky little
devilfish."

Tasi soon realized they had reached the castle
gates. The consequences of her actions suddenly
became real. She was immediately filled with dread.
Her father was going to be furious.

Kelix lead Tasi into the Great Hall, a cavernous
room constructed from the hulls of sunken ships.
The vaulted ceiling was made of sea glass and
fortified by massive titanium beams. It was an
ancient room. A royal room. It had a special way of
making anyone swimming through it feel very, very
small.

The floor of the room was made from polished

obsidian, as shiny and black as the deep itself. A mosaic in the center was made from little pieces of *alexandrite*, the realm jewel, along with abalone shell and pearls. The mosaic formed the image of an elaborate compass, the realm's sacred symbol. There was an inscription in the ring of gold around the compass. Tasi knew its meaning though it was in an ancient dialect no longer spoken in the realm. It was the realm motto she often heard the Collectors say in unison before their missions: *"Find the Lost."*

Tasi's heart was heavy. She knew she was a disappointment to her father. Today's incident would only make it worse. "No one is more lost than I am right now," she thought to herself.

A raised platform was at the head of the Hall. It supported two massive thrones carved out of bright orange sun coral. A spectacular red crest of sea fan spread out behind the royal heads. Tasi's father King *Zhāng Jié* was seated on the larger throne. She could see Fān's echo shell in his hand. Queen Jiāo, Tasi's kind stepmother, sat next to him.

Tasi approached slowly and bowed deeply at the foot of the thrones. She waited in that position for what seemed like an eternity before she heard her father's booming voice say, "Rise."

Tasi kept her face down, afraid to see the look of disappointment in his eyes.

"Tasi, your actions this day have caused the loss of valuable materials. You are guilty of trying to sabotage a royal mission according to the charges," the King began.

"Sire, if I may…" Kelix interjected in Tasi's defense.

"I wasn't trying to sabotage it," Tasi blurted out. "I just saw this incredible tusk lodged in the planks and I was trying to…"

The King, infuriated by this outburst, rose up out of his seat. Electric stingrays, sleeping under the King's throne, suddenly shot out, sending crackling electricity along the floor of the Hall. The shock caused everyone to jump.

"Out! I need a word with my insubordinate daughter," the King boomed. "Alone."

Everyone quickly cleared the room, as the Queen stood and gently touched the King's arm. "It's all right," he reassured her. "Go ahead and check on the little ones in the nursery." The Queen nodded and exited quietly, leaving the room feeling hollow and still.

The King took a deep breath. He swam over to a beautiful pink pearl, about the size of a puffer fish, mounted on an intricate pedestal. He gently touched the pearl, his face suddenly lost in memory.

"This belonged to your mother, Tasi. It was part of the family jewels she brought with her into our union. I treasure it because it reminds me of the blush that would come over her cheeks when she was tickled by some secret thought. I always hoped she was thinking about me in those moments. She was holding you in her arms the last time I saw it."

Tasi swallowed hard. Her father rarely spoke of Queen Jenai, her mother. It felt strange to imagine the three of them as a family.

"Soon after," the King continued, "that rogue wave destroyed our nursery and took her away from me forever."

The King turned and approached Tasi. He lifted her chin so she was looking into his eyes. "Your mother gave her life so you would survive. Nothing in this realm is more important to me than you, Tasi."

The King put his hands on Tasi's shoulders as he continued, "You are 15 years old. You need to honor her now – and the rest of our royal family. You cannot be sneaking into the outer realm and chasing after foolish things."

The King could see the conflict on Tasi's face and wondered what would cause his daughter to disobey the rules. "Tell me, what was so important in that shipwreck?"

Tasi tried to sound casual but soon her voice was filled with passion. "Some truly unique treasures I can use in my creations," she said. "They make my work look neat, Father, and I really do think they make other merfolk feel happy."

"Nothing, no matter how unique, is worth the life of my daughter," the King said, unimpressed by her explanation.

TASI

"I just wanted to make you proud. I thought these things would set my work apart – like yours did when you were my age. They say you were the most gifted engineer in the realm," Tasi told him.

"But my work strengthened the secret bridges that connect our entire city," the King clarified. "Mariana merfolk build things that make our city stronger. They don't make things that *look neat*."

The way the King used Tasi's words against her stung. She had hoped her father would understand her inventive side. It was obvious now he never would. Tasi hung her head. She was crushed.

"I'm sorry to have to do this, Tasi, but until further notice, you are officially on restriction. You may not leave the city under any circumstances," the King told her. "Focus on your classes if you want to be like me. Remember what they say in school? 'We find, fix and form together, so....'" The King waited for Tasi to finish the catchy slogan.

Obediently, Tasi mumbled, "...so Mariana can last forever." Tasi asked to be dismissed. She felt numb and defeated. She hurried to escape the judgment that seemed to fill the entire Hall.

4

Faithful Friends

Tasi rushed back to her quarters and locked herself inside. She was overcome with sadness. Slowly, she turned around and noticed Copper rising up out of her kelp bed. She was relieved. She opened her hands and Copper swam happily into them.

"Oh, Copper! I am so glad you are here," Tasi exclaimed. "It seems you are the only one who understands me." Tasi began to cry. She had to be careful to control her sobs or else the entire city would hear her. Mermaids can project their cries for quite some distance if they want to, just as whales do. Sometimes it just happens.

Copper began to swim around excitedly, causing Tasi to look up and take notice. "Oh goodness!" she said, backing up. Tasi's entire room was aglow! The details in her art sculpture, the decorations on her walls, the embellishments in her kelp bed canopy and Copper's custom armor, all pulsed with ethereal light.

The ability to make things glow was Tasi's special power. It was a gift she only recently discovered she had, so she was still figuring out how to control it.

The power had flowed easily from Tasi's joy and excitement until now, as she created things and helped others. But, seeing her entire room aglow today gave her a better understanding of her gift. "I didn't know I could do this with sadness," she admitted to Copper. "I guess my secret ability is tied to extreme feelings."

Copper began to do a silly little dance for Tasi that lightened her mood. She giggled, reaching out her hands to her faithful friend. "You're right, Copper. Let's try to keep the glow power connected to happiness from now on."

It was no fun to be on restriction. But Tasi knew if she hadn't done the right thing today, she never would have learned the secret to mastering her gift of light, and she may have lost her dear friend Copper forever.

Tasi went into her Form and Function class the next day with a much better attitude knowing she could make anything more unique with her glow powers. Building things seemed a whole lot more exciting.

The classroom was a large space. It was filled with projects of all kinds. There was a massive steel

door fitted with numerous sample hinges, knobs and window work on it. This is what they were studying the other day before Tasi was sent out to repair the hinge for old Mrs. Chow.

The ceiling was crisscrossed with replicas of the secret bridges that stretched across Mariana. Students floated along the high expanse with various tools, such as blowtorches and sheets of metal. They repaired any cracks or weaknesses their teacher would create when no one was around.

Their teacher's name was Master Héng Zhǐ, which meant "lasting and wise." He was both of those things and more, given the fact he refused to ever retire. The students treated him with much respect but mainly because they were afraid to cross him.

Master Héng Zhǐ noticed Tasi enter and turned his back. It was a sign he was disappointed in her behavior yesterday. Tasi took a deep breath, trying not to let it bother her, as she turned towards the rest of the class. They already were gathering for the day's lecture.

Tasi spotted a cheerful face in the group, with cheeks so round and rosy they nearly made her eyes disappear when she smiled. It was her best friend Mira, waving eagerly at Tasi to join her. She quickly made her way over, no longer wishing to be the target of Master Héng Zhǐ's disappointment.

"Where were you yesterday?" Mira asked, tucking one side of her short black hair behind her ear. "I couldn't find you after our community assignment."

"I finished early with Mrs. Chow, so I went to check out that shipwreck Kelix was telling us about," Tasi confessed. "It didn't go like I planned." Tasi lowered her eyes and pursed her lips for a moment, remembering her difficult talk with her father.

Mira's eyes grew wide as she asked, "Did they see you following them?"

"Well," Tasi began. "I kind of caused part of the ship to collapse, so yeah. They saw me. Kelix tried to protect me, but Fān made sure I got in trouble with my father."

"She's trying to make sure you never leave the realm again," Mira said.

"I know," Tasi agreed.

"That's so she can have Kelix all to herself," Mira said with a smirk.

"What do you mean?" Tasi asked, innocently.

"She is in love with him, but he only has eyes for you," Mira explained. "So if she can get you out of the way, then she'll be able to make her move."

Tasi threw her head back and laughed. "Wow, do you have a wild imagination," she told Mira. "Kelix is just a friend who can't keep a secret when it comes to great adventures. He doesn't… *like* me," Tasi insisted. But thinking back to how Kelix stood up for her in front of the King, made a lump rise in Tasi's throat. She shook it off. It was a ridiculous idea.

5

Back to Work

S uddenly, the whole workshop blazed with electricity. Glowing fingers of energy zapped along the metal beams in the room until the voltage hit rock and exploded into sparks. Some of the students shrieked in surprise, as the rest of class immediately quieted down.

Master Héng Zhǐ turned around. Behind him was a cage filled with electric stingrays, the same kind of beasts that slept under the King's throne. The Master had just fed them some small fish; and when the rays used their electricity to stun their food, wires in the cage conducted the energy throughout the workshop.

"Mariana is the deepest and darkest realm in all of Oceana," the Master began. "But it is filled with strength and power because its people know how to harness the energy of the deep."

Master Héng Zhǐ floated over to a series of pipes. "This energy not only comes from living creatures," he explained. "What else lurks beneath our city?"

The students looked at each other. Was there a bigger monster down there none of them knew about? That's when Mira's hand shot up. The Master gestured for his top student to enlighten the group.

"It's lava," Mira answered.

The Master nodded his head. "Lava from the greatest force in our realm, Dà Hēi," he said with a reverence for the massive undersea volcano that made the entire class silent and wide-eyed.

"Many tubes and vents connect to Dà Hēi that keep us warm," the Master told them. The students nodded their heads, thinking of the smaller vents located near many of their homes.

"They are called 'black smokers.' We are connected to one right here in our workshop," the Master said, gesturing to the pipes. "The heat from the black smokers can be used to melt down the nodules and other metals we collect, so our realm builders can make repairs and build new structures."

The Master picked up several hunks of metal. He raised them high, so the class could see the difference.

"Not all metals are created equally," he began. "Some are strong and hard, such as iron. Others, like aluminum, are weaker and more flexible. They also are quick to melt and easier to use."

The students nodded their heads. They were accustomed to working with steel in the workshop. Steel comes from iron.

"Today, we are going to learn how blending certain metals can give us the best of both qualities," Master Héng Zhǐ said, as he placed the iron and aluminum into a large cauldron connected to the top of the pipes.

The class began to murmur amongst themselves about what was going to happen next. A great rumble beneath the floor caused them to fall silent in anticipation. It was an earthquake. These were practically an everyday occurrence in Mariana. But, the students were not used to seeing the force of the quake force harnessed to melt metal.

The quake caused the lava in the underground rivers to rush through the tubes. Bubbles filled with searing heat began to gush towards the surface as the hot lava mixed with the cold water. The Master's pipes started to vibrate with the force of the rising heat. They grew hot and red.

The students could see the metals melting and sinking into the bowl – first the softer aluminum and then finally the iron. Master Héng Zhǐ rotated the cauldron, mixing the metals together.

"What we have now is no longer iron or aluminum. It is something new," Master explained.

"It's better for many things because it is now both strong and flexible."

Master Héng Zhǐ then tipped the great cauldron so the new metal blend poured out into a large mold that extended out towards the students. They watched as the molten metal filled the squares and cooled.

"When we work together we are stronger and better than when we are alone, just like this metal," Master instructed. "So pair up and take a sheet to the welding stations. Let's see what you can create with this."

6

Better Together

Tasi and Mira took their sheet of metal over to their workstation. "We need to make something that reflects our strongest talents," Tasi said, thinking out loud.

"I'm not really a creative person," Mira told Tasi. "I'm better at solving problems."

Mira spotted a large crack in the secret bridge structures. She floated up to the ceiling. "Other people might try to just patch this. But see how the crack is coming from movement between these two sections of the bridge?" she pointed out. "A patch is just going to come loose."

Mira returned to the workstation and began to roll and twist her sheet of metal into a strong cable. She hammered the edges flat as she explained her concept to Tasi.

"A better tactic would be to make metal cables, like this one, and attach them to either side of the crack," she said, returning to the bridge. She stretched the cable across the break and hammered large spikes through the flat edges into the bridge. "The bridge can still move a little bit if you do several more like this. But the pieces don't fully come apart and merfolk still can travel along them."

"So, it's kind of like stitches you get from a doctor?" Tasi asked.

"Exactly," Mira confirmed.

"That's brilliant," Tasi exclaimed, feeling proud of her friend's solution.

"What will you do on our project, Tasi?" Mira asked with an encouraging tone.

Tasi didn't have to think about it. She began to wrap copper wire, adorned with pearls, around Mira's cable.

"Is that making it even stronger?" Mira asked.

"Maybe a little," Tasi guessed. "But I'm doing it to show that your cable is special and meant to last. It isn't just a quick fix." Tasi continued to embellish as she worked. "I am turning our work into something merfolk can feel proud of by adding valuable and beautiful elements."

Mira cocked her head as she studied Tasi's creative touches. "Tasi, you are an artist!" she said. A huge smile spread across Tasi's face as she considered the title. "I guess I am."

A gravely cough startled the girls. It was Master Héng Zhǐ standing right behind them.

Mira and Tasi quietly stepped aside so the

Master could evaluate their work. He reached out and tugged at Mira's cable. It was strong, but had a good amount of give to it. He grunted with satisfaction.

The girls exchanged a look of happiness. That was about as close to a compliment anyone ever got from the Master. He then gently touched Tasi's copper and pearl adornments and his brow knit into a curious expression. Tasi wasn't sure if he liked her work or not.

The Master finally spoke after a few moments of silence.

"Once there were two mermaids. One had very strong character and the other had great beauty. Which one made a better wife?" he asked.

The girls looked at each other. The answer seemed obvious. "They both would be good wives," Mira replied.

"...for different reasons," Tasi added. "But their value is equal."

A slight smile touched Héng Zhǐ's lips as he asked his next question. "What about after many cycles have passed?"

The girls stared at the Master blankly. They did not understand where he was going with this lesson.

"Beauty fades," he said, answering his own question. He reached up and touched Tasi's adornments one last time. He turned back to the girls and said sharply, "Invest in strength."

TASI

"Good work, Mira," he added as he glided away to evaluate the next group's work.

Mira quickly searched Tasi's expression. She didn't want her friend to feel bad. But Master Héng Zhǐ's snap judgment only made Tasi feel bold.

"Forgive me, Master. But I think you forgot something," Tasi blurted out. "What about the third mermaid?"

The Master turned back, intrigued. "The third?" he asked.

"Yes." Tasi said. "You told us about two mermaid wives – one strong, one beautiful. But you forgot about the third wife who was strong *and* beautiful. She was really the best wife of all."

Tasi put her arm around her friend. "When we work together, we can have the best of both, can't we?"

There was a long pause. Then Master Héng Zhǐ grunted. He turned and floated away.

The girls threw their arms around each other and swirled in a circle. Mira's eyes were bigger than ever. Even her cheeks couldn't hide them this time. "I can't believe you, Tasi," she exclaimed. "You are as brave as you are talented."

They both looked after Master Héng Zhǐ as he graded the next team with another one of his stories.

"You are going to get an 'A' in this class," Mira said. "Or you are going to get expelled!" The thought made both girls giggle.

The students dutifully put away every tool into its rightful place at the end of class. This was part of the Form and Function philosophy. "Take care of your tools and they will take care of you," the Master always said.

They also cleaned up every leftover piece. Mariana merfolk never wasted anything. They were naturals when it came to recycling, especially where metals were concerned. Scraps always could be melted down and formed into something new.

Master Héng Zhǐ would normally float around the room, like a shadow of responsibility, ensuring that every workstation was spotless. But today, something strange happened. The Master approved Tasi's station as usual and turned to leave. That's when Tasi noticed something under his tail. She glided over to see what it was once he had moved on.

There, on the floor, was a spool of copper wire and a collection of pearls just like the ones she had used to adorn her project with Mira. It was a gift – a silent gesture of approval from the Master. Tasi picked them up and clutched them to her chest for a moment, daring to believe that her talent may some day be valued in the realm.

7

Secret Bridge Hangout

Tasi and Mira sat up on the secret bridge after class, happily munching on kelp chips. They talked about graduate placements – a ceremony that happened for all young merfolk after they finished Form and Function. They graduated and were placed into the community according to their talents if they passed the course.

"I want to be a Collector," Tasi announced.

Mira giggled. "Sure you do. That way, you can have your boyfriend escort you to the ends of the realm and back."

"What boyfriend?" Tasi asked.

"Kelix, of course." Mira said with a smirk. "But you'll have to get rid of Fān first."

Tasi shook her head. "Here we go again with your crazy imagination."

"I know," Mira continued. "Maybe you could

lead her out to the *Lùsè Shíkū* and throw some glowing moss on her and a mackerel shark will eat her up."

Tasi gave Mira a playful shove. "That is a horrible thought!"

"Fān is a horrible mermaid," Mira retorted. "I'm pretty sure the law says 'anyone interfering with royal true love shall be fed to the sharks' or something like that," Mira said with her finger in the air, trying to sound official.

Tasi tried to hold back her laughter. "I'm beginning to think you're the one in love with Kelix, the way you talk about him all the time!" Tasi teased.

Mira shook her head confidently. "The truth will come out, Tasi. What is lost is always found."

Tasi decided it was time to change the subject back to Mira. "So what is it that you want to be after placements?" she asked.

"I still don't know," Mira confessed.

"Well, you said it yourself, you're good at solving problems. You should train to serve on the high counsel," Tasi suggested.

Mira laughed and shook her head. "Only the best and brightest get to advise the King," she said.

"That's what you are!" Tasi insisted. "Besides, I think I know someone who could put in a few good words on your behalf with his highness."

"Maybe we should wait until after you are done being in trouble," Mira joked.

"True," Tasi agreed, as she munched another chip. "I don't know if I can stand it, Mira. I can't go anywhere. Where am I going to get treasures for my projects?" Tasi flopped back on the bridge, feeling all the fun had drained away from her life forever.

Mira stared down and caught a glimpse of a black smoker. She had an idea. "You know how good I am at solving problems?" she asked. "I think I know a way for us to have an adventure without having to leave the city."

Tasi perked right up. "See! I knew you'd make a great royal advisor. Now advise me before I die and dry up like one of these chips!" Tasi gleefully demanded.

"We could explore the lava tubes," Mira said. They run all along the bottom of the realm.

Tasi thought Mira had lost her mind. "How

can we explore tubes filled with lava? We will get burned alive!"

"No," Mira explained. "Many of the tubes are empty. They were created by the lava flow that has cooled in the water. They aren't dangerous anymore."

Tasi listened, trying to imagine going down there. "So, we squeeze into the tube and then…" she began.

"No squeezing," she said. "These tubes are like giant tunnels. The best part is they are filled with minerals, like moonstone, gold, quartz…"

Tasi shot up into the water. "Enough," she exclaimed. "You had me at moonstone. I'm in!" She swirled in the water, but then stopped herself short. "Wait. Can Copper come? He always comes with me to find treasure."

Mira laughed. "Of course. It wouldn't be an adventure without him."

8

Tube of Wonder

Mira lead Tasi and Copper down to the bottom of the city. The light all but vanished from the world above as they descended. Lamps, filled with bioluminescent ooze, projected from the sides of the buildings, giving the streets an eerie glow. The water became even colder and fewer and fewer fish could be seen darting about.

"It's pretty creepy down here," Tasi said, pulling Copper in close to her side.

"Dangerous, too," Mira admitted. "Many things grow to unbelievable size in the dark. That's why the young merfolk don't explore the depths alone."

Mira pulled a coral rod out of her satchel and swam over to one of the lamps. She swirled the rod in the glowing ooze, making a torch light.

"This will help us find our way." Mira led Tasi even deeper.

TASI

They came to the mouth of a lava tube. Tasi could see in the dim light of Mira's torch this was no tiny tube. It was more like the mouth of a cave. The water inside was icy cold and blacker than the night.

"Maybe we should come back with a few more torches," Tasi suggested, her fear making her voice shake a little. Copper darted back and forth in agreement.

Mira's face turned towards Tasi in the glow and said one word, "Moonstone." She smiled brightly, took Tasi's hand, and headed bravely into the

cavernous tube.

Mira swam over to the wall of the tube and brought her torch in close. Tasi could see the markings where the lava had once flowed. She could see veins of minerals, copper, nickel and gold! Tasi took the chisel out of her pack and began to mine flecks of the precious metals into a collection bottle. She turned to show Mira what she had collected.

But Mira was staring at something else. Tasi followed her gaze, squinting her eyes to make out the shape. There was a faint glow deeper in the cave. It was beautiful. Purple and green lights were dancing in the dark. Tasi was mesmerized.

"Copper, wait!" Mira shouted. That's when Tasi noticed Copper was swimming towards the lights. Tasi instinctively dashed after him. Soon, Tasi and Copper were close to the dancing lights. They seemed small and magical and safe. Tasi reached out her hand to give one a little touch.

Mira swooped in with her torch. The thing that was dancing with such beauty was suddenly illuminated. What it was attached to wasn't beautiful at all.

Huge jaws filled with pointy teeth gaped in front of Tasi's face. Hollow white eyes searched blindly for prey. It was a *footballfish* that had grown utterly giant in the depths, and must have stretched over nine feet long. The only thing pretty about this monster was the glowing lure dangling inches away

TASI

from its lethal jaws.

Tasi raced backwards, fearing for her life. She couldn't escape. The walls of the tunnel had her trapped. She began to pound her fists against the walls, overcome with panic.

Suddenly, the entire cave was filled with bioluminescent light. The veins of minerals pulsed with it and the hidden gems glowed like stars in the milky way. Both mermaids gasped in wonder.

The massive footballfish floated deeper into the cave, unable to sense where they were. Mira watched it pass to a safe distance. She turned to Tasi.

"What is going on?" she asked.

Tasi looked around at the bright light and realized her panic had made this happen. Copper swam to her side, excited by the powerful display. "It's just like the other day in my room," she said to Copper.

"You did this?" Mira asked.

"It seems to happen whenever I have a strong emotion," Tasi started to explain. "Copper and I were just trying to figure it out, and…"

"You never told me about it?" Mira asked. She was upset. "I thought we were friends." Mira turned her back, trying to deal with rising pangs of jealousy.

"Mira, it's all so new, I just…" Tasi said, calling after her.

Mira turned back around with a hurt look on

her face. "I actually worried about you. I thought 'How is poor Tasi going to find her place because all she wants to do is art?'" she said, sounding angrier than ever. "Here you have one of the most powerful gifts in the realm!"

Tasi swam close, wanting to put her arms around Mira and somehow make her understand how confusing all of this had been. But Mira pushed her hands away.

"You don't need me, Tasi. You already have everything. You're a royal daughter and you're a *luminist…*"

"A what?" Tasi interrupted, not understanding the word Mira just used.

"Ugh!" Mira snapped. "Go ahead and keep your precious secrets!"

Mira whirled around and swam away.

9

Alone in the Darkness

Tasi allowed herself to sink to the bottom of the tube. She buried her face in her hands. How did this adventure go so wrong? She didn't know this ability to make things glow was a mermaid power.No one ever told her this might happen.

"Why was Mira so angry, Copper? That's just not like her," Tasi asked, as Copper swam in close. "I'm not trying to be different. I'm trying to fit in."

In an effort to cheer her up, Copper swam over to a gem imbedded in the wall of the tube and did his little happy dance for her.

"I don't feel like collecting right now, Copper. I just want to go home," Tasi said. She rose back up in the water. The glow inside the tube began to fade. Tasi guessed it would be wise to use the light to find their way back out.

Tasi and Copper were faced with the darkness

of the depths once outside the tube. She searched the water for signs of the lamps, but couldn't see anything. That's when she remembered her compass. "The compass always will lead us back to the castle," she said opening the lid.

The compass immediately started to glow, empowered by Tasi's hope. But a compass is a small thing and its glow in the deep was little more than a candle against a vast dark night.

Tasi followed the compass' magnetic needle. The water began to feel a little bit warmer. "I think we are getting closer to home, Copper. I feel a heat vent."She swam deeper, hoping to find the source, thinking she could follow the bubbles back up to the city.

"Look!" Tasi said as she came down on top of what looked like another tube. Tiny holes in the tube were emitting bubbles. "This one still must be filled with lava," she told Copper, as she used the compass glow to follow along the tube's length. They unexpectedly reached the end of the tube.

"How is this possible?" Tasi asked as she searched the end. It was completely blocked off, as if old lava already had flowed along this path and cooled. "This tube is old, but the lava inside of it is fresh. It has nowhere to go."

The sea floor shook. An earthquake! It was much larger than the one Tasi felt earlier in class. The movement caused a deep crack to appear at the blocked end of the tube. The buildup of lava inside

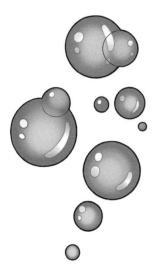

pushed against the crack causing a rush of super-heated water to burst forth. The bubbles sent Tasi and Copper tumbling backwards.

Tasi screamed! The bubbles had burned her scales. She swirled in the cooler water to ease the pain. Then she looked for Copper. She could see the tiny glow of his armor approaching her in the water. Soon, he was close enough for her to see that he was fine.

"Thank goodness for your armor, Copper!" she cried with relief. Copper examined Tasi's arms, trying to see how badly she had been burned.

"I'll be okay. Let's just follow these bubbles up and find out where we are exactly," Tasi suggested, leading Copper back towards the tube. They rose slowly with the bubbles. But what they found at the top made Tasi gasp. It was the castle nursery!

"Oh my gosh, Copper. My family is in danger. One more large quake and that tube is going to crack open. Tons of lava will leak into the water all at once. The wave of hot bubbles will burn everyone," Tasi exclaimed with fear. "I have to warn my father!"

10

Dangerous News

Tasi found the King in his meeting room with several of his advisors. She burst in, but then paused in awe. She never had actually been inside this room before. It was off limits to those not carrying out official business.

The entire room was made of pearls. The glowing torches in the room were reflected in the pearls, making the entire space incredibly bright. Tasi remembered her father saying the meeting room was one of his favorites. "It's easy to see clearly what I must do when I am inside this room," he had told her.

Tasi thought her father was referring to how his advisors helped him see what to do. She now realized the King was also talking about how literally bright the room was. "It *is* easy to see in here," she said out loud.

The King looked up with a furrowed brow. He did not tolerate being interrupted. But, Tasi was gushing with the news of the danger before he could react. She told him all about the blocked tube and the searing bubbles. "We have to hurry before the next earthquake hits!" she passionately explained.

Advisor Xuē leaned in towards the King and whispered something in his ear. The King nodded. "Xuē is right," her father then announced to the group. "This kind of blockage is quite common in the tubes. The lava builds up, then breaks out and forms a new tube. It would have to be very close to pose any real danger."

"This tube is right under the castle nursery, father," Tasi pleaded.

Advisor Dá then pulled out a map of the lava tube network. "We keep track of all the tubes and their growth, little one," Dá explained as he pointed out the tube near the nursery.

Tasi peered down at the map with the others. She could see that each tube was not only marked, it was named. The tube under the castle was called "Wò Lóng," which meant Sleeping Dragon.

"Wò Lóng has grown since you last took your measurements," she explained. "It is much closer now."

"Perhaps we could just drill a few vents in the tube to release the pressure?" Xuē suggested.

"No!" Tasi blurted out. "The pressure is already

too high. The workers will get burned."

Xuē began to chuckle. "What do you really know about it, child?"

Tasi thrust out her arms to show her burns. "See for yourself!" she shouted in frustration.

Her father's hands were suddenly on Tasi's shoulders. He led her towards the door. "Tasi, trust that we will take care of this," he said gently. He gestured to one of the attendants standing by the door. "Guard, please escort my daughter to the nurse to tend to these burns."

She dutifully allowed herself to be lead away. She wanted to trust her father, but she could not dismiss the panic she felt rising in her chest.

Tasi's arms were wrapped in "kombu" in the nurse's chambers. These sea vegetable leaves were rich in minerals and would help her scales recover. She was then left alone to rest.

She opened her eyes after a brief nap to discover Mira at her bedside. "Mira," Tasi said with glad surprise. "I thought you were going to be mad at me forever."

Mira chuckled, but then became serious. "I'm sorry I left you in the deep, Tasi. I don't know what came over me," she said, trying to explain. "I think I was feeling really jealous about your new power. Then I felt like a total fool for worrying about you all the time."

"It's okay, Mira," Tasi began. But Mira cut her off again.

"It's not okay. You're my best friend. I feel like it's my fault you got hurt," she said. "I am so sorry."

Tasi smiled, accepting Mira's apology. "I'm sorry too. I should have told you about my glow powers," she added. "It's like Master Héng Zhǐ always says: We are better when we work together."

Mira nodded and smiled back. But the vision of the lava tube rushed back into Tasi's mind and she sat up with a start. "We have to get out of here!"

"You need to rest," Mira said, trying to make Tasi lie down again.

"No," Tasi insisted. "I saw a lava tube about to explode right under the castle nursery. I told my father, but he didn't believe it was that serious. We have to fix it right away!"

"Leave it to me," Mira said. "I will go and make sure the realm builders are working on it."

"What if they're not?" Tasi asked, fear visible on her face.

"Then I will get Kelix and the entire royal guard to help us!" Mira promised as she swam quickly out the door.

TASI

11

A Royal Decree

Mira returned with Copper and Kelix by her side. "Nothing is being done, Tasi," she announced.

"The guards have received no word of this danger or any repair missions," Kelix added.

"You are right. That tube will explode with lava when the next large quake hits," Mira confirmed.

"Then it's up to us," Tasi said, as she got up out of bed.

"But what about your burns?" Mira asked, as Copper flitted about in concern. "Don't you feel the pain?"

"I'm worried about my family," Tasi explained. "The only thing I feel is… brave!"

She began to formulate a plan as she swam towards the door. "We're going to school."

Mira, Kelix and Copper were confused. But they followed her to the Form and Function workshop anyway, as Tasi explained her idea.

"Do you remember how Master Héng Zhĭ taught us about this new metal blend that was both strong and flexible?" Tasi asked. She showed them the sheets the Master had poured out into the molds.

"Mira used this metal to make an awesome cable to fix a crack in the bridge," Tasi said as she swam up to the bridge to show off Mira's work.

"You want us to make a bunch of these for the tube?" Mira asked, starting to understand the plan.

"Yes," Tasi said. "Kelix will get the guards to crisscross these cables over the blocked end of the tube."

"But lots of cracks will occur when the quake hits. How will we know where to put the cables?" Kelix asked, not following the logic.

"We want the cracks," Mira explained. "The lava needs to get out."

"But we don't want it to get out all at once," Tasi said, finishing the thought. "We just need to prevent an explosion."

"Great!" Mira exclaimed. "We will get working on these cables while Kelix rallies the guards."

Kelix started to leave, but then paused. "How am I supposed to get the Cerberi to do this?"

"Tell them this isn't a repair mission, it's a *royal decree*," Tasi said, and then added: "An emergency, too!"

A small quake suddenly shook the workshop,

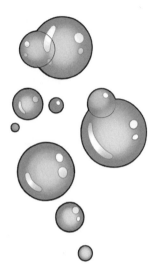

causing the black smoker to fire up. Tasi poured the metal elements into the cauldron to melt. She turned back to her friends.

"I can make decrees, too. I am a royal daughter, after all." She said with enough confidence to send Kelix racing off to the Cerberi.

Tasi turned to Mira with a look of worry after pouring the molds. "I've done the calculations," she said. "I don't think we have enough metal to make the number of cables we will need."

Mira paused, trying to think of a solution. She floated up to the secret bridge and looked at the original cable she and Tasi had made. She tugged on the cable.

"Maybe we could make our new cables thinner

in order to stretch our resources," she thought to herself. "But then they wouldn't be as strong."

Then, Mira ran her fingers over Tasi's embellishments.She considered the copper wire and the stones. "Maybe Tasi's artistic touches are more than just pretty," she realized. She dashed back to Tasi's side.

"I have an idea!" she said, her dark and sparkling eyes as wide as ever.

"Of course you do," Tasi said with a grin. "You're my royal advisor!"

The two mermaids just smiled at each other for a moment. Tasi broke the silence.

"Go ahead… advise me," she said.

"We are going to need the treasures from your chambers," Mira said.

Tasi's happy expression faded. "This is no time for art," she said.

"Together we are strong and beautiful, remember?" Mira said with encouragement. "Now go get those treasures."

Tasi paused, thinking of the mountain of goods she stashed inside her chambers. "All of it?" she asked.

"All of it," Mira said with confidence. "But don't bring it here. Meet us at the lava tube."

Kelix returned with the Cerberi just as Tasi was preparing to leave.

"Perfect timing," Tasi said. She addressed the guards, mustering as much authority as she could.

"You know your mission. We must act quickly. Help twist these cables and deliver them to the mouth of Wò Lóng."

The guards looked at each other, puzzled. "Wò Lóng, your majesty?" one asked.

"That is the name of this tube – the Sleeping Dragon," Tasi replied. "But it won't be sleeping much longer. Hurry!"

The guards quickly dashed to the molds. They pulled out the metal sheets as Mira instructed them on how to form the long, thin cables.

Tasi turned to Kelix. "You're with me," she said, as she and Copper dashed towards the door. A silly grin spread over Kelix's face as he turned to follow.

TASI

12

Trouble at the Tube

Kelix helped Tasi and Copper deliver all the treasure she had collected to the lava tube. But Tasi made an alarming discovery when they got there. None of the work was being done! Mira quickly swam to her side.

"We have a problem," Mira said as she pointed to a group of merfolk speaking to the Cerberi. It was the Collectors. One mermaid was doing all the talking – Fān!

Tasi clenched her fists, as she swam down to the group. "Why the delay?" she asked the guards. "You have your orders."

Fān swam to the front of the group. "What orders?" she asked in a sneering tone. "I hear talk of a royal decree, but I don't see any documents. Where is the royal seal?"

Tasi could feel her mind racing. There had to

be a way to shut Fān down. "This is an emergency. Things are handled differently when the royal nursery is in danger," she said.

"Why did the King put a 15-year-old princess in charge if it is so important?" Fān asked, trying to sound innocently curious. She turned to the guards with her blow. "I think the authority of the royal guards is being manipulated for a school project."

Fān swam over to the chief of the guards. "What do you think the King will say when he finds out you are wasting time and resources on a dead lava tube?"

Another quake rocked the trench. This one was even stronger than the one before. Tasi pushed past Fān to the guards.

"What do you think the King will say when he finds out you ignored the royal decree and allowed his family to be burned?" she asked with plenty of power and authority.

"I get it," Tasi said, gesturing to the Collectors. "These workers are wise and we trust them to gather our resources. But Fān is just a Collector. I am a Royal Daughter of Mariana."

Tasi picked up the end of one of the cables. "Help me defend the future of our realm."

The guards rallied with a cheer, stretching and drilling the cables across the closed mouth of the Sleeping Dragon. Tasi immediately set to work wrapping the cables with her treasures. She used the strands of copper, nickel and gold, studded with gems and stones of all kinds, to fortify the cables.

Fān, angry at being dismissed, turned to leave. She noticed she was alone. All the other Collectors decided to stay and help. She whirled around in a huff and sped towards the castle.

"We'll see what the King has to say about this," she said with a hiss.

13

The Dragon Awakes

A huge earthquake struck the city as Fān entered the Royal Great Hall. The castle groaned. The great walls trembled. Pieces of the intricate ceiling fell loose and plummeted through the water to the mosaic floor. Fān could see the Queen racing towards the royal nursery. The King caught sight of Fān. He swam quickly to her side.

"Have you seen my daughter?" he asked, his brow intense with worry.

"She is following your orders, Sire," Fān answered, waiting to see the King's response. He stared at her in confusion. Fān knew in that moment that Tasi had made up the royal decree. She had been right!

But that didn't seem to matter anymore as she saw the King's concern for his little girl. Fān no longer felt jealous of Tasi. She realized that Tasi was trying to do what was right for everyone in Mariana… including her.

"Tasi is at the mouth of Wò Lóng," Fān told the King. "She's trying to protect the realm!"

The King took his chamber guards and rushed towards the danger of the deep. He couldn't believe his eyes when he arrived.

All of the Cerberi and the Collectors were standing back from the blocked tube, which was now a mass of angry cracks. A network of glowing bioluminescent cables was holding the end of the tube together. Lava pushed its way out of the gashes, sending searing pipes of steam towards the surface.

The King saw the pipes were small. Pressure was escaping without burning any of his subjects. An explosion had been averted.

The quaking finally stopped. The guards and the Collectors saw the cables were still holding. They let out a cheer of joy and relief. The King floated over to Tasi's side.

Seeing her father made Tasi instantly bow her head. Now she was going to have to answer for her royal decree.

"I'm sorry I did this without your permission," she said softly. "I knew our family was in danger and I couldn't lie in bed and do nothing."

The King took a deep breath. "You know, Tasi," he began. "I did something very similar when I was your age. I thought my father was going to punish me. But, you know what he told me instead?" The King asked. Tasi shook her head.

"Right now I see less of what you have done and more of who you have become," the King said, quoting his father. "He didn't make me wrong. He eventually made me King."

Tasi raised her eyes to meet her father's gaze. She saw tenderness there, not anger.

"Tasi, I used to hope you would be a lot like me. Today, I see you are exactly like me. I couldn't be more proud."

Tasi looked around at all the merfolk she had rallied to her cause. She saw Fān in the middle of them. The expression on Fān's face was finally one of admiration and respect. It was a pretty amazing thing she had done.

Mira, Kelix and Copper saw Tasi's gladness and relief and swam to her side. Tasi then gushed to the King about how they all had helped solve the dangerous problem.

"I see you already have your own advisors, guards and friends," the King observed with a smile.

"Together we made something that really works," Tasi proudly said.

The lava surged in the tube, causing all the gems, stones and glass wound around the cables to to glow. The light, enhanced by Tasi's biolumines-cence, was utterly dazzling.

The King took Tasi's hand in his own with a

gasp.

"Oh, it's more than that," he confessed to his royal daughter. "It's beautiful."

Mariana Glossary:

1. **Alexandrite:** the realm jewel for Mariana. It's a precious gem that changes colors with light, alternating from blue green to purple and red.

2. **Bioluminescence / Bioluminescent:** light created inside living things. Eighty to ninety percent of deep ocean animals have this ability to glow.

3. **Black Smokers:** hydrothermal vents coming from underwater volcanoes that exist all over Mariana.

4. **Cerberi:** the name given to the Royal Guards of Mariana.

5. **Collectors:** special units of Mariana merfolk assigned to scavenge the realm for important artifacts needed for building and maintaining the city.

6. **Copper:** Tasi's Sea Buddy. Copper is a tiger tail sea horse, common to Malaysia and the Philippines. Tiger tails are vulnerable because they are highly prized for Chinese medicine. Tiger tails are masters of camouflage, and can change color to blend in with their surroundings.

7. **Dà Hēi:** a huge and famous volcano in the northern part of Mariana, known on land as Daikoku.

8. **Footballfish:** a type of anglerfish that only lives in the deepest parts of the ocean. The footballfish is a large fish with jaws lined by razor sharp teeth that lures its prey in with a single glowing antenna on its head. The glow temporarily hypnotizes other fish, so the footballfish can eat them before they know they are in danger.

9. **Hǎinán Wān:** the area known as "Shipwreck Bay" by the Mariana people. Hǎinán Wān is a famous dive site in the Philippines. Humans call it "Coron Bay," and divers from all over the world travel there to explore. It is famous for its Japanese shipwrecks from World War II.

10. **Lǜsè Shíkū:** the green sea plains outside the Shēn where the Mariana merfolk get all their medicinal seaweed.

11. **Mariana:** the oldest realm of Oceana. It is located in the Pacific Ocean near Guam and the Philippines. It stretches between Japan in the north, covers the China Sea, Malaysia, and Palau, and ends at Australia.

12. **Mìmì Qiáo:** the "secret bridges," or passageways that connect the city. These bridges are created from the tops of undersea mountains that have fallen to the ocean floor during earthquakes. The Mariana people use them as short-cuts and roads.

13. **Shēn:** the capital city of Mariana where castle Zhēnzhū lies. The location of the Shēn is known on land as the Mariana Trench. The Shēn is the deepest spot in the entire ocean, descending over 35,000 feet. The trench is so deep and treacherous it is virtually impossible to explore by humans.

14. **Zhāng Jié:** the King of Mariana, Tasi's father.

15. **Zhēnzhū:** the castle of Mariana, located in the Shēn. Its name means "pearl."

Tasi

- Royal Mermaid Daughter of the Mariana Realm
- Name means "ocean"
- Has fiery red hair and green eyes
- Has a shimmering tail of electric purple
- Special powers are bioluminescence (*the ability to make things glow*) and camouflage (*the ability to blend in with her surroundings to avoid danger*)
- Special talent is her artistic ability to add "sparkle" and make practical things beautiful
- Father is King Zhāng Jié (*pronounced "Zahng Jee·eh"*)
- Home is the Castle Zhēnzhū (*pronounced "Zun·zoo"*), which is made from the remnants of sunken ships and rises majestically out of Challenger Deep

Copper

- Tasi's Sea Buddy
- A rare tiger tail seahorse
- Special ability is camouflage (*the ability to blend in with his surroundings to avoid danger*)
- Wears custom armor designed by Tasi
- Helps Tasi create art and hunt for unique treasures

MARIANA

Mariana Realm

- The oldest of the 12 realms in the world of Oceana
- Realm symbol is the compass
- Realm colors are gold, electric purple and purple-black
- Realm jewel is the color-changing stone Alexandrite
- Realm motto is "Find the Lost"
- Is a dark, dimly lit realm because it is so deep
- Contains many great buildings and other fantastic creations made of all kinds of metal
- Includes the mysterious Mariana Trench that lies east of China and the Philippines
- Has steep gorges that plummet to the deepest parts of the ocean
- Is connected by caves and cleverly lit pathways called Mìmì Qiáo (*pronounced "Me·me Tchee·ow"*)
- Has a northern province called Hǎizhēn (*pronounced "Hi·zun"*), which stretches from the top of New Guinea to the East China Sea
- Has a southern province called Hǎiyáo (*pronounced "Hi·yow"*), which includes the South China Sea and the waters off Indonesia and Malasia
- Is connected to the Ryukai (*pronounced "Ree·yooh·ka·hy"*) Realm near Japan by the Hei Chao (*pronounced "Hay·Chow"*) River, a warm underwater current that brings life to the coral reefs

TASI

COPPER

To purchase another

ENCHANTAILS™

SLUMBER BAG SET

ENCHANTAILS™

LUCIENNE Slumber Bag

ALSO INCLUDES:
• EASY CARRY TOTE • DECORATIVE PILLOW •
• COORDINATING WALL DECALS •

www.enchantails.com

The Adventures Continue...

Lucienne is an adventurous mermaid who often forgets she's a Royal Daughter. She regularly gets into trouble for her escapades. She tries to relate to the other mermaids of the Grileglas Realm, but doesn't feel she fits in. One day she meets a boy named Leo, an outcast in the realm. Leo belongs to a dangerous merpod of leopard boys who find adventure in seal racing. Lucienne and Leo think their friendship is harmless until Lucienne's Sea Buddy, a Gentoo penguin named Prince, becomes bait for the next seal race. It's up to Lucienne to save Prince in time. Will Leo honor their friendship and help Lucienne? Or will he side with the leopard boys and allow them both to become trapped?

Visit www.enchantials.com to:

SHOP for more great stories
BUY an Enchantails Slumber Bag Set
LEARN about Oceana's Realms & Royal Mermaid Daughters

Dive Into Other Realms...

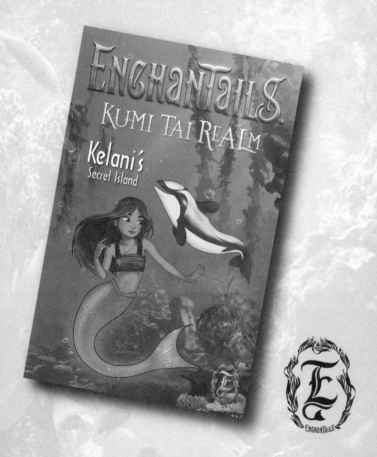

Kelani is a kind, free-spirited royal mermaid who seeks out adventures on her secret island. A deadly adventure interrupts her usual peaceful visit to her hideaway with her Sea Buddy, Keiki an endangered Maui dolphin. Uninvited guests discover her lagoon and begin to destroy the island. Kelani makes an unlikely friendship, and faces her greatest fear in the form of air-breathers (humans). Can Kelani save her island? Can she keep her realm a secret? Or, will the air-breathers ruin her island and expose her world?

Visit **www.enchantials.com** to:

SHOP for more great stories
BUY an Enchantails Slumber Bag Set
LEARN about Oceana's Realms & Royal Mermaid Daughters